The Flight of the Buzby Bee

The Flight of the

Buzby Bee

by David Lyon

Published by Ernest Lyon Media Productions
P.O. Box 26101
San Francisco, California 94126-6101

ISBN 0-9741328-0-2

Printed and bound in China by Regent Publishing Services, Ltd.

Library of Congress Control Number: 2003093465

www.flightofthebuzbybee.com

This book is dedicated to anyone who has ever wondered
what it was like to be a bee, and to those who have not;
to those who have actually been a bee for a short period of time;
and to those who still are.

Once up in a tree, there was a hive where lived one hundred bees.

And one of these bees was named Buzby Bee.

Buzby liked to spend his days at outdoor cafes, playing guitar, harmonica and tambourine.

And just like all the other bees, Buzby was deeply in love with the Queen.

One day, the Queen called all of the bees together, and told them of a special garden, where the sweetest of flowers bloomed.

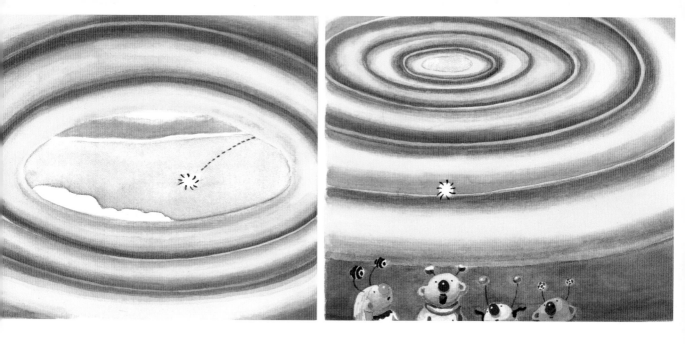

She asked for a brave volunteer to visit this garden and fetch some nectar to make some honey for her crumpets and tea.

A nervous silence fell upon the hive. Buzby wanted to go but he was too shy to say so.

At just this moment, a small fluff of pollen drifted inside, and floated slowly down, until it landed upon the tip of Buzby's nose, where it tickled and itched, and itched and tickled, until Buzby sneezed -- "Achoo! -- and stumbled forward.

Suddenly, everybody was looking at Buzby!

Buzby was about to explain that he had only been sneezing, when he saw the Queen smiling down upon him very proudly.

Buzby bowed low. "I would be honored," he said, "to fetch some nectar for the Queen!"

And then all the hive began to buzz.

Buzby watched three bees perform a beautiful dance which told him where to find the flower garden.

And then he set off, past hills, and streams, and valleys, and beaches, using only his notes to guide him.

But when Buzby landed in the garden, none of the
flowers were blooming, except for a single dandelion.

"What's going on?" Buzby asked. "These flowers are
supposed to be in bloom!"

"Somebody picked one of their friends yesterday," said
the dandelion. "These flowers will not bloom until their friend
is returned."

"But I need some nectar for my Queen!" Buzby said.

"The flower is in that yellow house," explained the
dandelion. "Rescue the flower and you will get some nectar."

"Brother!" said Buzby, but he picked up his bucket and flew straight towards the house. He was just about to fly inside when -- BAM! -- he hit something hard and invisible and tumbled down to the ground below.

Buzby lay there for quite some time until he was awakened by a beautiful creature floating above him and shining with light.

"Are you my guardian angel?" Buzby asked.

"No, I'm just a garden-variety firefly," said the Firefly. "And you had better get up or someone is going to step on you!"

"But I need to get into that house!" Buzby said.

"I have a friend who might be able to help you," the Firefly said, and she led Buzby to an old tin can, inside of which someone was singing a love song about garbage.

When Firefly knocked upon the can, a strange-looking bug appeared.

The bug poked Buzby in the chest, and asked, "Now who might you be?"

"Why, I am a bee!" said Buzby. "I am a bee; a bee, I be; de bee you see, de bee is me! Buzby Bee at your service!"

"Far out," said the bug. "Well, I am Fly. Fly on the ceiling and on the wall; fly in the kitchen and down the hall; fly in your soup and fly in your ointment; I fly where I want to; I don't need an appointment."

Firefly explained to Fly what had happened when Buzby tried to get into the house.

Fly chuckled, "That's a window, Bee. Windows are nothing. I can get you inside!"

Fly showed Buzby and Firefly how to sneak inside the house.

By the time they got to the flower, however, it had collapsed upon the table.

"We must get this flower back to the garden or it will surely die!" said Firefly.

Buzby, Fly and Firefly lifted up the flower, and carried it back to the garden.

Buzby and Fly carefully attached the flower back to its roots, while Firefly fluttered overhead, shining light down upon them.

Then Buzby, Fly and Firefly
lifted the flower up. At first,the
flower wobbled in the breeze, but
when the rays of the sun shone upon its
face, it stretched its leaves and smiled!

When the other flowers saw that their
friend had been saved, they burst into
bloom, in a great spectacle of color,
light and sweet perfume, laughing
and joking in the breeze.

Buzby figured this was a good time to ask if he could have some nectar.

"Please!" said the flowers. "Take as much as you wish!"

Buzby gently gathered all the nectar he needed, thanked the flowers and then said goodbye to his new friends, Fly and Firefly. Buzby promised that he would visit again as soon as possible.

"Yes, and maybe we can meet this Queen of yours," Fly said, and then they all hugged goodbye.

Buzby raced home.

The Queen was in her chambers when Buzby returned. Buzby bowed low and presented the nectar to her. Honey workers immediately took the nectar and turned it into a special honey.

The next morning, the Queen invited Buzby for breakfast to enjoy some of the honey with crumpets and tea. The Queen thanked Buzby for his hard work and bravery and explained that she wished to give him a reward.

"Well, I was hoping you might go with me to the garden and meet my new friends," Buzby said.

The Queen did not know what to say. She wanted to go, but she was not sure if this was the sort of thing that a queen should do.

At just this moment, that same old fluff of pollen floated slowly down to the tip of the Queen's nose, where it itched and tickled and tickled and itched, until she sneezed -- "Achoo!"

"Is that a 'yes'?" asked Buzby.

"I think it is," said the Queen.

And then all the hive began to buzz.